LEGO® friends

Andrea Takes the Stage

By Sonia Sander

Illustrated by Pixel Mouse House LLC

SCHOLASTIC INC.

ISBN 978-0-545-51756-0

12 11 10 9 8 7 6 5 4 3 2 1
Printed in the U.S.A.

MIX
Paper from responsible sources
FSC   FSC® C020056
www.fsc.org

13 14 15 16 17 18/0
40

First printing, September 2013

Mia, Stephanie, Olivia, and Emma came to see Andrea at the City Park Café.

4

The friends each got to work. Stephanie and Andrea made invitations.

This looks perfect!

Meow!

CONCERT
CITY PARK
CAFÉ
7:00 PM
FRIDAY

Oops! Kitty, you stepped in the paint.

We'd better wash your paws.

With Kitty all cleaned up, Stephanie copied the invitations.

Purrrr.

BEEP! BEEP!

Then the girls drove all over Heartlake City to deliver them.

Olivia had the plans for the stage done in no time at all.

What do you think, Goldie?

Tweet! Tweet!

The girls headed to the City Park Café.

Let's start building!

We're ready to roll!

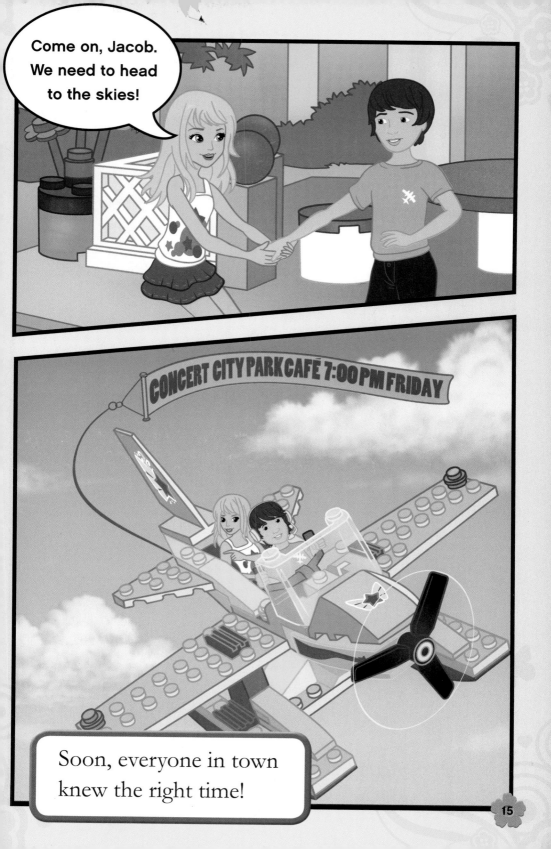

With one more mess avoided, Andrea put on her dress.

Testing, one, two, three . . .

You look *and* sound great!

Suddenly, the power went out!

BZZZZT!
BZZZZT!

We can't have a show without lights and sound.

It's an easy fix . . . if I can find the fuse box.

Olivia got to work on the fuse box.

Just a few more switches and we'll be all set.

24

Emma quickly sewed pieces of star fruit onto the dress.

Almost done!

Hurry, Emma— the show's about to start!

Thanks to her friends' help, Andrea was ready to take the stage.

My new song goes out to my friends, who made this party happen.